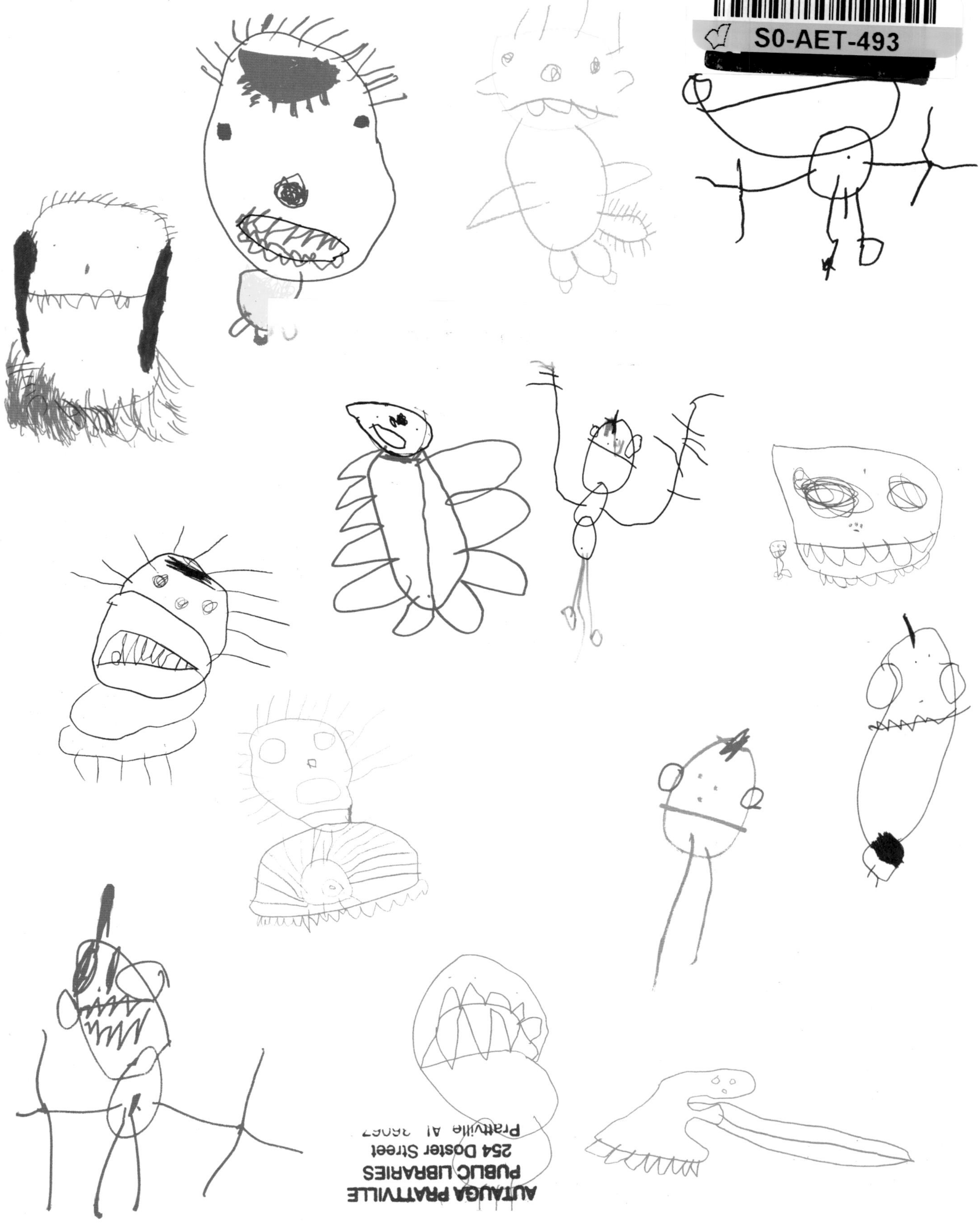

Lewis Trondheim

Monster Mess

Jean · Dad · Kriss · Petey · Mom

PAPERCUTƵ ™
New York

MONSTER #2 "Monster Mess"
"Monstreaux Bazar," volume 1, Lewis Trondheim
Copyright © 1998 Guy Delcourt Productions. All rights reserved. English Translation Copyright © 2012 by Papercutz. All rights reseved.

Thanks to Pierre and Jeanne for the monsters.
Thanks to Brigitte for Pierre and Jeanne.

Lewis Trondheim — Story, Art, & Color
Joe Johnson — Translation
Michael Petranek — Lettering
Janice Chiang — Logo
Adam Grano — Production
Michael Petranek — Associate Editor
Jim Salicrup
Editor-in-Chief

ISBN: 978-1-59707-294-6

Printed in China
January 2012 by PWGS
Block 623 Aljunied Road #07-03B
Aljunied Industrial Complex, 389835

DISTRIBUTED BY MACMILLAN
FIRST PAPERCUTZ PRINTING

Our names are Petey and Jean.
We're kids.

We play.

And we play a lot.

We cry
a lot, too.

And when there's a cartoon DVD
on, we're really good.

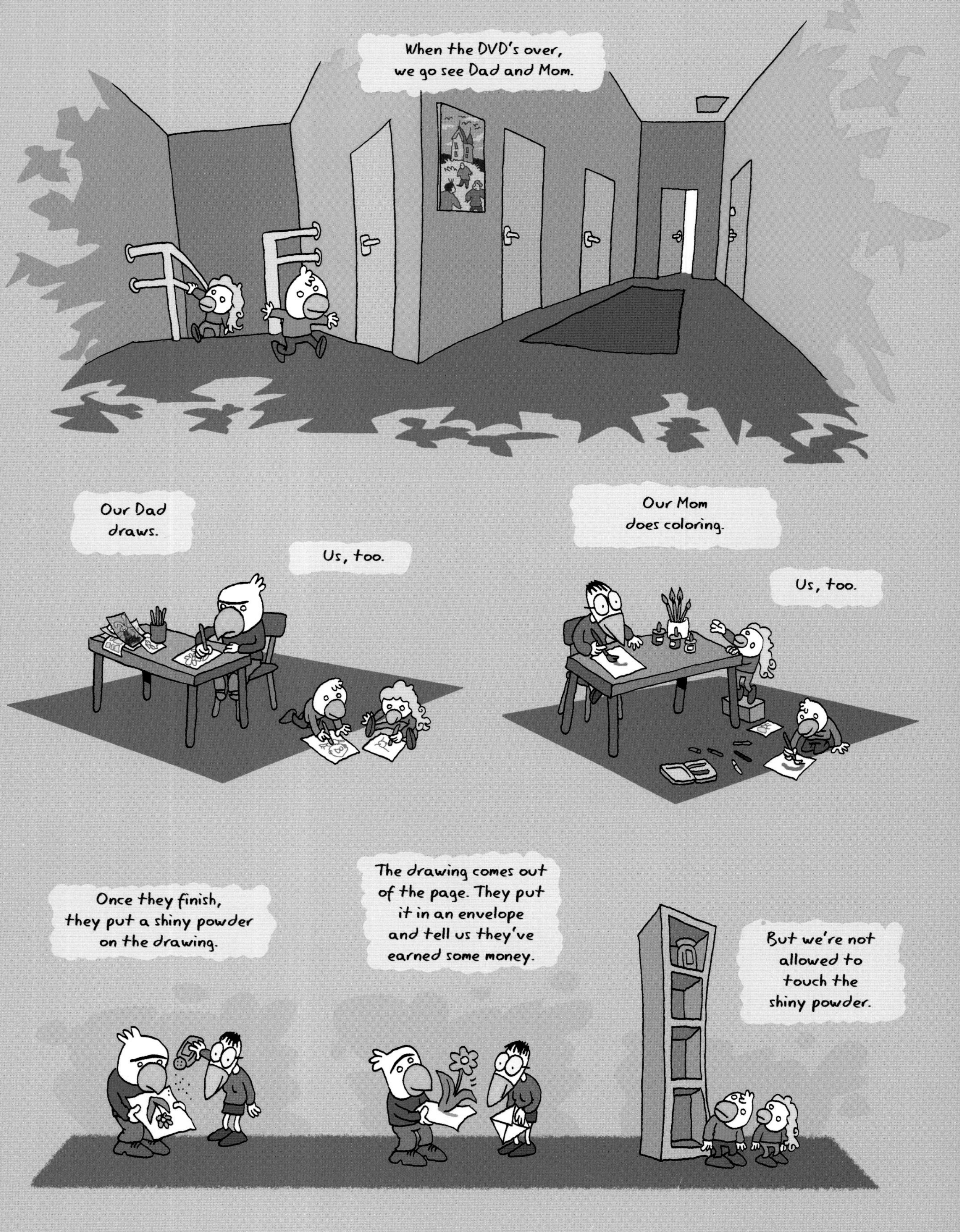
When the DVD's over,
we go see Dad and Mom.
Our Dad
draws.
Us, too.
Our Mom
does coloring.
Us, too.
Once they finish,
they put a shiny powder
on the drawing.
The drawing comes out
of the page. They put
it in an envelope
and tell us they've
earned some money.
But we're not
allowed to
touch the
shiny powder.

We're not allowed to make our drawings come out of the pages.

But our drawings are pretty, too.

We make tons of nice looking monsters, with lots of arms and teeth.

And afterwards, we give them names.

BLOBLO

GOMGOM

BAGABAGA

KRADAK

SAPATE

OKO

Red is good for drawing mouths... so sometimes we tussle over the red pencil.

But we make a mistake. The shiny powder falls on Oko.

We quickly go hide in our bedroom.

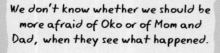

Oko is afraid, too, and he hides behind the leg of a table.

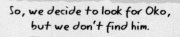

We don't know whether we should be more afraid of Oko or of Mom and Dad, when they see what happened.

So, we decide to look for Oko, but we don't find him.

6

Suddenly, Oko leaps towards us, and gets ready to eat us.

Luckily, he has teeth made of paper, and it doesn't hurt us very bad.

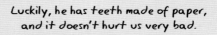

But it really scares us!

We quickly go see Mommy and Daddy and cry and tell them everything.

We're happy we don't get a spanking. And afterwards, we're sad because Mommy and Daddy don't find Oko.

They say he could be anywhere.

"There are two solutions," says Daddy. "The first is to move away and leave this house."

But we don't want to move away. We have all our toys here.

"The second solution is to draw a nice monster to eat the bad monster."

We like that.

"Okay... let's say he'll have three legs to chase after monsters, four arms for catching them, ten mouths for eating them."

"And two teeth for biting them."

Our mom asks us what we want to call him, so we say "Kruduk."

But dad says no, nice monsters need a real first name.

So, we call him "Kriss."

He looks nice.

But he's a little clumsy.

Dad tells him to go look for Oko and to eat him. Kriss heads straight to the kitchen.

And he eats everything in the fridge... even the carrots and spinach.

Mom asks him if Oko was in the fridge, and Kriss answers that he doesn't know, but that he was hungry.

Afterwards, Kriss has fun with us. We laugh a lot.

Dad looks for the broom, but he doesn't know where it's been put away. By chance, he finds the vacuum and says it'll do the trick.

So, he chases after Kriss and tells him to go eat Oko. Otherwise, there'll be a problem.

He even says he won't repeat himself twice... and that means that Dad is really mad.

Kriss starts looking for Oko.
Dad watches him a little,
then he comes back to us.

"We just have to wait,"
says dad, while sulking.

Rather than wait, mom says she's
going shopping again. We go with her.
That'll keep us from staying with dad
while he sulks.

And also, when we do our shopping,
there's the baker-woman who
sometimes gives us candy.

When we arrive at the
supermarket, people run away,
but we're not making
faces at them.

Mom says she understands why
once she sees Kriss in the aisles
devouring everything.

Kriss gets really scolded by Dad.

Even that time when we painted on the walls, we didn't get scolded like that.

Dad says it's frustrating, that he should have drawn a more intelligent, more obedient monster.

So, Kriss gives Dad a big hug and tells him that his ten mouths aren't hungry anymore now and that he can look for Oko for real.

Dad wipes off Kriss's slobber, which is all over his face. We laugh.

To have a laugh, too, Dad pretends to chase us to give big, wet kisses.

We laugh again, because Dad's not mad anymore.

Afterwards, we make a drawing of Oko on paper so Kriss can spot him easier.

He looks hard for Oko everywhere and stops messing around.

Since Oko is tiny, he can hide anywhere.

Anywhere, really.

We get tired just watching Kriss running around in every direction.

We hope he'll find the little monster quickly, so he can play with us afterwards.

That's when we hear Kriss shouting. He must have found Oko.

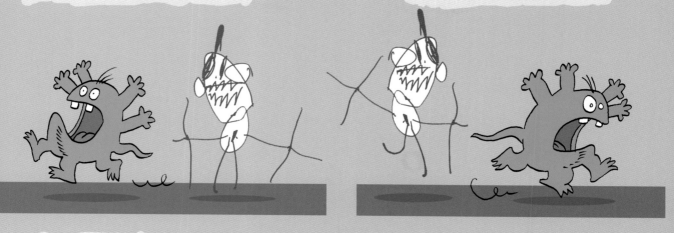

But Kriss is the one who's afraid, actually.

He says Oko has gotten really, really big.

Dad's not happy. He says he'll take care of it himself and that only Kriss's foolishness is "very, very big," and, what's more, that you don't run down the stairs.

Dad goes and sees Oko, then he comes back shouting and running down the stairs.

Dad says that Oko must have eaten some paper to have gotten bigger like that.

He also says that "sparks are gonna fly." We don't know what that means, but sparks are gonna fly, that's for sure.

"And this time," says Dad, "I'm going to use the supreme weapon!"

We bring Dad the plastic sword, but he says that's not the supreme weapon and that he's going to go get it.

We think Dad has some bombs hidden somewhere, but he comes back with a glass of water.

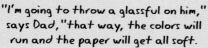

"I'm going to throw a glassful on him," says Dad, "that way, the colors will run and the paper will get all soft."

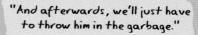

"And afterwards, we'll just have to throw him in the garbage."

On the way, Dad gets thirsty and drinks the glass of water.

Then he finds himself facing Oko, but he no longer has any water to throw on him.

He quickly comes running back.

Dad goes back to see Oko with a glass full of water. He's still a little thirsty but, this time, he doesn't drink any.

He throws the glassful at Oko, but Oko bends away and the water passes to the side.

Oko laughs and says that dad won't escape this time.

Dad tries to escape anyway, and Oko pounces on him.

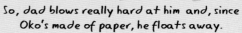

So, dad blows really hard at him and, since Oko's made of paper, he floats away.

Dad has time to rejoin us. He wonders what we'll do to get rid of Oko.

Mom has an idea. She says that Kriss could put water in his ten mouths and spit it on Oko. He couldn't miss that way.

So, we say we could all put water in our mouths and spit it on Oko.

But for once when there's something interesting to do, Mom tells us no.

Kriss asks if water won't make him disappear, too.

Dad answers that Kriss was drawn with water-resistant inks, and Oko was drawn with erasable markers for children.

So, Kriss says okay. He starts putting water in his mouth, but he spits it all back out.

He says that water is gross, that he's willing to do it, but with lemonade instead.

So, we give him some lemonade.

His mouths are full of it. It makes him look like a smashed frog we saw one day on the side of the road.

Since we say so out loud, it makes Kriss laugh. And then we see he no longer has any lemonade at all in his cheeks. He'd already swallowed everything.

Afterwards, he very much needs his three legs to avoid Dad hitting him with the vacuum.

We hear noise upstairs.

Mom says that this can't go on and that we all have to go up there.

Mom fills two pots for herself.

Dad takes some bottles of water and a mouthful, too.

We'd like to put some in our mouths for spitting, too, but Mom says no and gives us some glasses.

Dad makes Kriss put some water in his mouths, even if he says he doesn't like it.

Then we all go upstairs.

Oko is going to have a heckuva surprise.

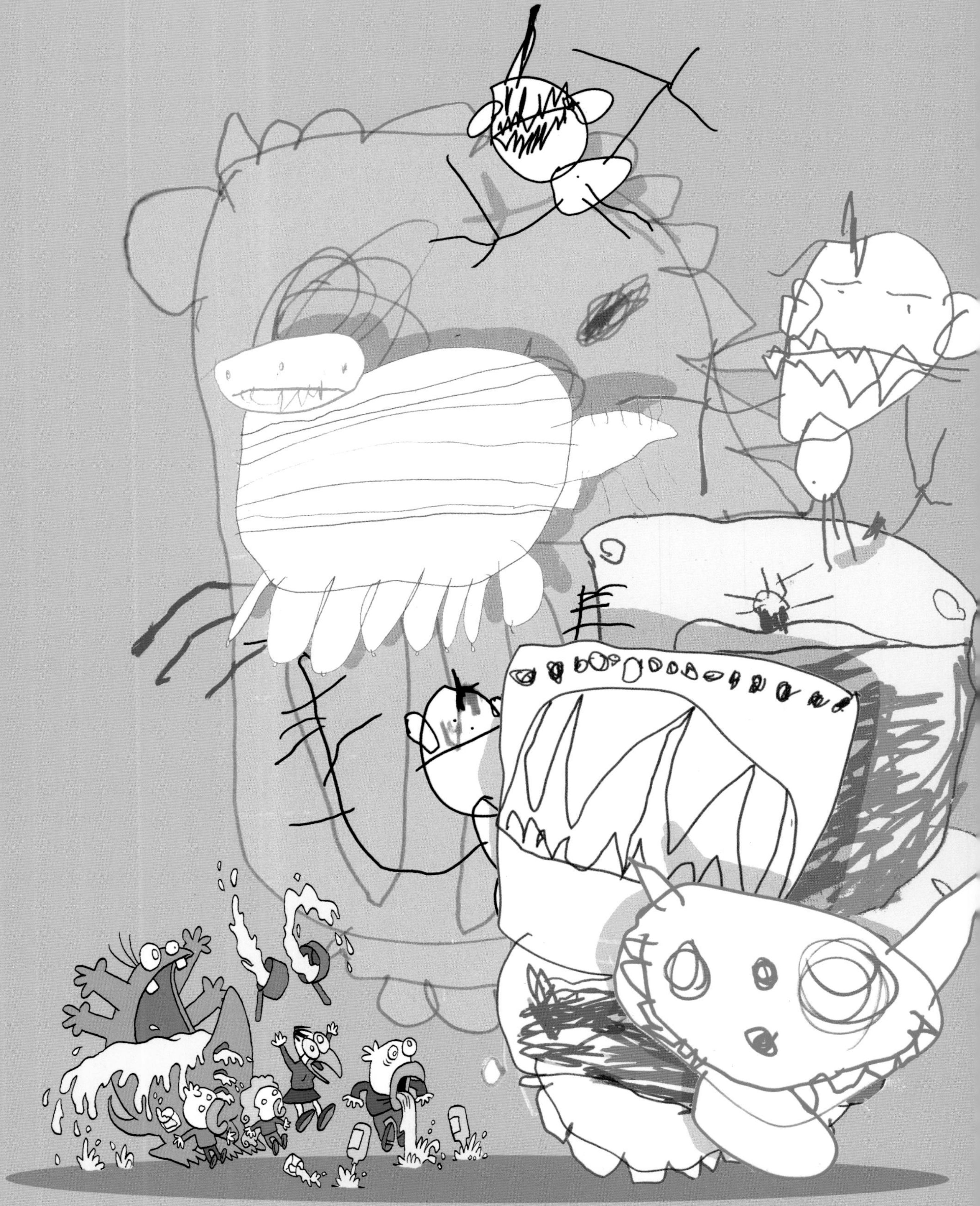

Oko has used the shiny powder to awaken the monsters we'd drawn.

We all run away really, really fast, screaming really, really loud.

But all the monsters chase us.

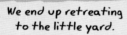

So, we scream even louder.

We end up retreating to the little yard.

We should be okay there.

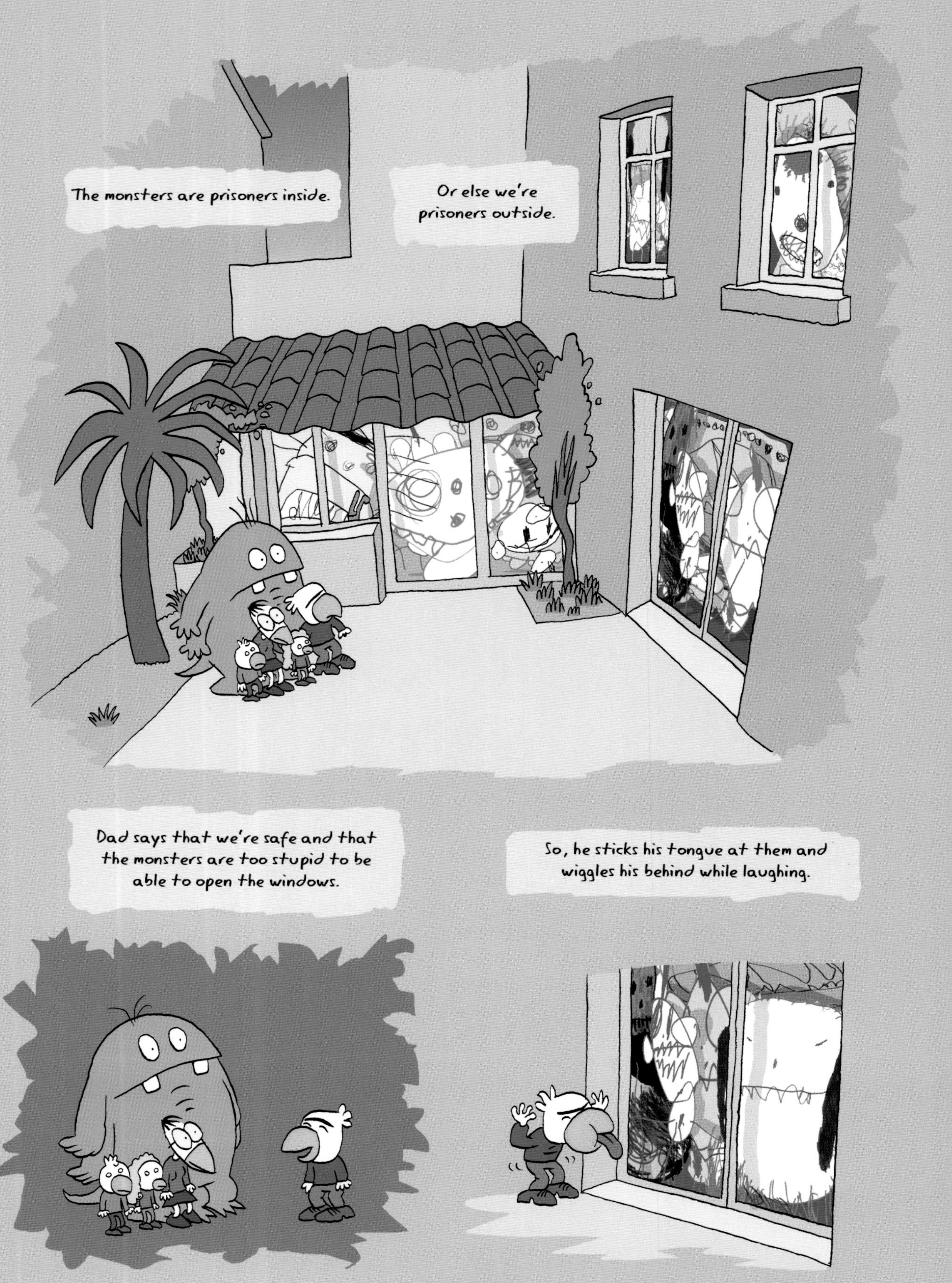
The monsters are prisoners inside.
Or else we're prisoners outside.
Dad says that we're safe and that the monsters are too stupid to be able to open the windows.
So, he sticks his tongue at them and wiggles his behind while laughing.

Mom tells him to stop, that it's a disaster. Dad answers that wagging his butt is no disaster.

Then he sees the monsters sliding under the window and he understands what Mom was trying to tell him.

This time we're completely surrounded. Oko laughs while looking at us.

Suddenly, Dad thinks of the garden hose!

But because he never puts it away right, the hose is all tangled and the water won't flow.

He doesn't have time to untangle everything. A monster leaps towards him.

Luckily, Dad sneezes just then, and the monster floats away.

Kriss helps us to climb onto the shorter roof, while dad spins the hose over his head to make the monsters back away.

Afterwards, he makes it twist around his head, and the monsters are no longer very afraid.

He quickly joins us on the roof.

The monsters do too, so we cross over to the neighbor's terrace.

They're having dinner.
Dad says a quick hello to them.

The monsters don't say hello to them.

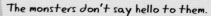

Mom says to follow her up
to the top of the roof.

And afterwards, she says we'll wait
for them there and that we'll
throw things on them.

So, we search for things,
but there's nothing on the roof,
nothing at all to throw.

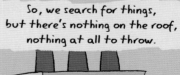

Here's the first monster coming!

Mom grabs one of dad's shoes and throws it right at the monster's head.

But the shoe tears the paper and goes right through.

Right afterwards, Mom throws the second shoe, and then the monster falls down to the little yard.

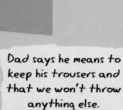

We don't have a moment to breathe before a new monster arrives, then another, and yet another.

Dad says he means to keep his trousers and that we won't throw anything else.

So, Mom says that we're going to throw Kriss on them.

We don't want to because Kriss might get hurt.

Mom says he has nothing to fear.

So, very, very bravely, Kriss closes his eyes and, all by himself, throws himself on the monsters.

And since all the monsters were climbing up the ladder then...

He smashes them all at once.

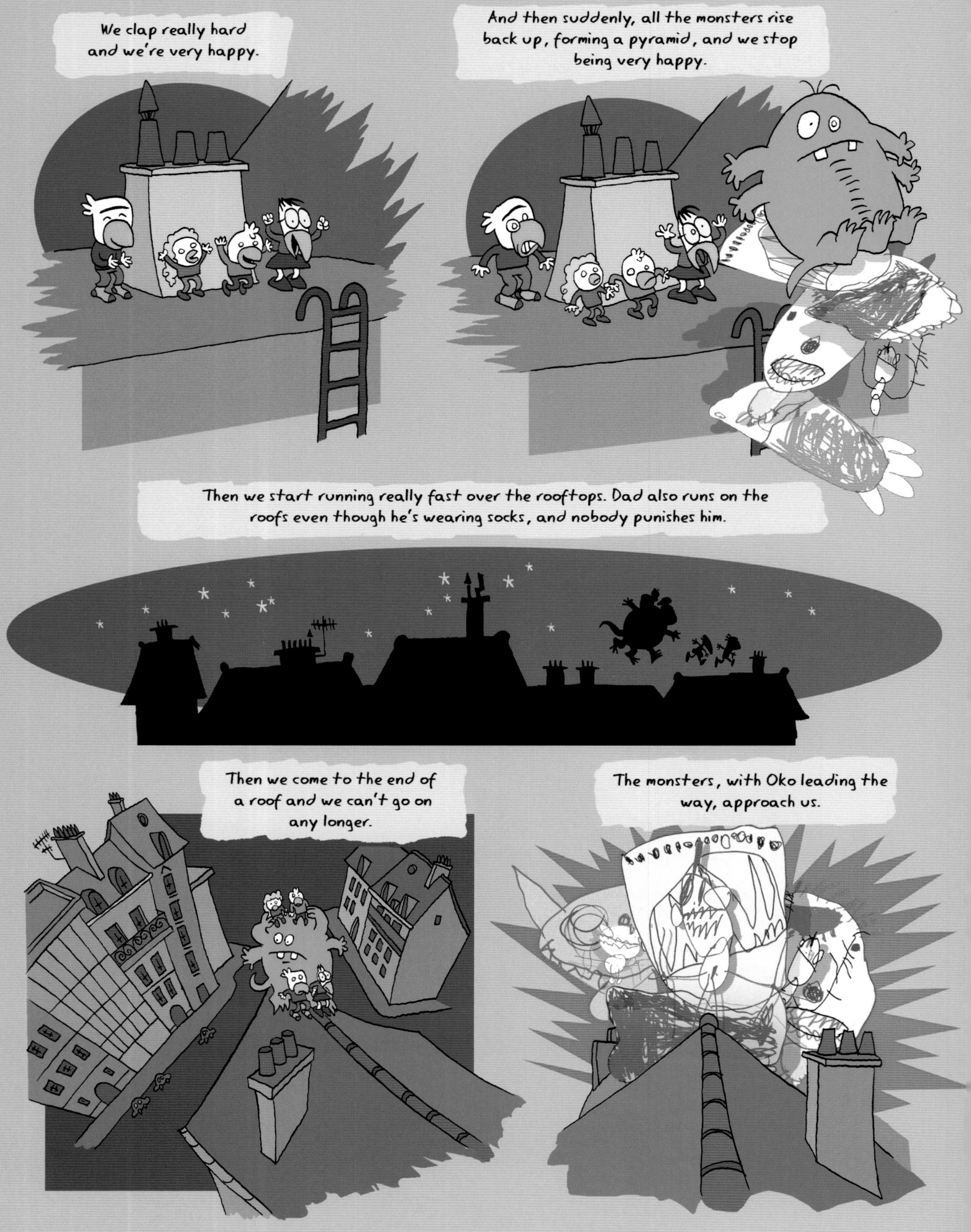
We clap really hard and we're very happy.
And then suddenly, all the monsters rise back up, forming a pyramid, and we stop being very happy.
Then we start running really fast over the rooftops. Dad also runs on the roofs even though he's wearing socks, and nobody punishes him.
Then we come to the end of a roof and we can't go on any longer.
The monsters, with Oko leading the way, approach us.

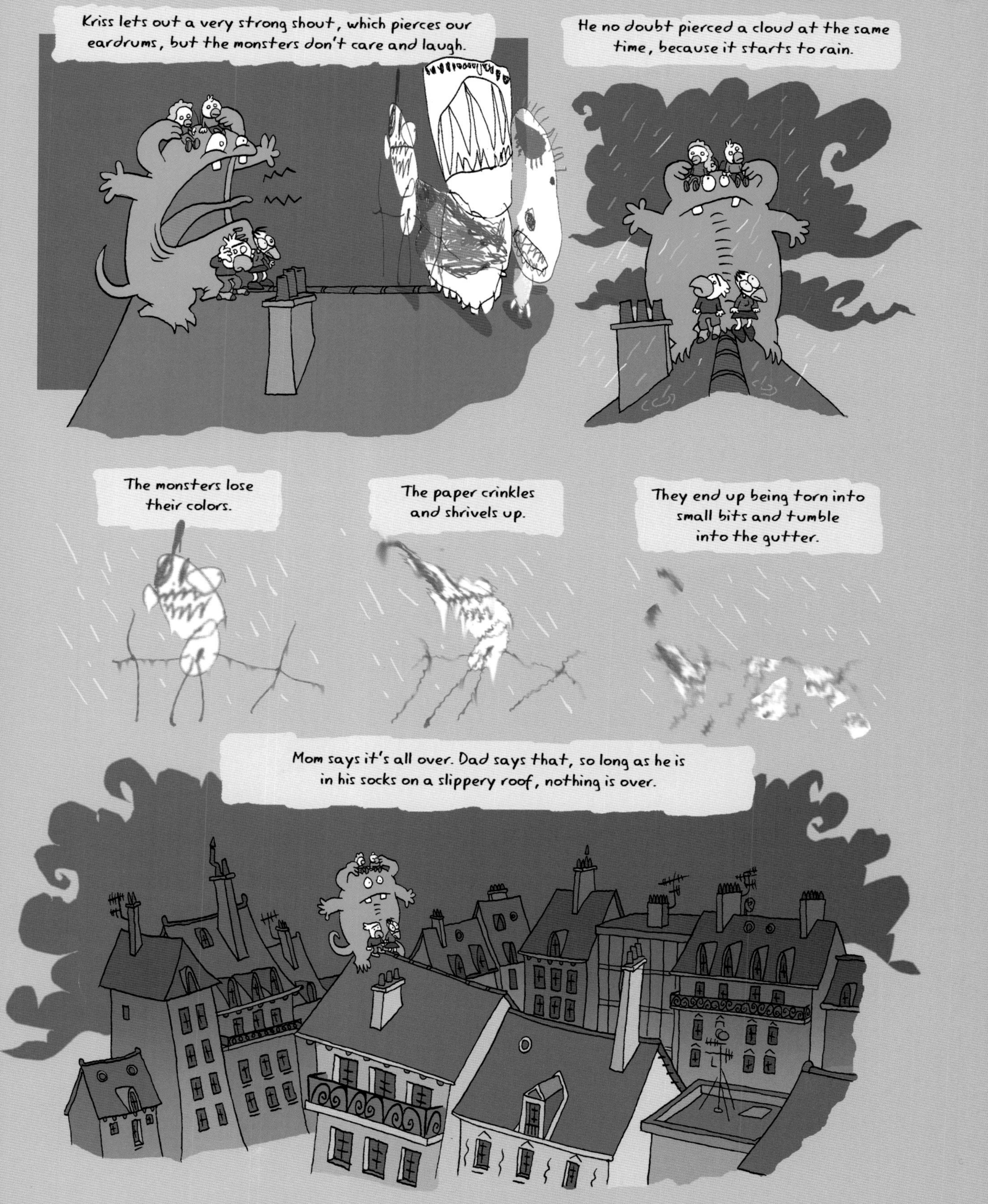
Kriss lets out a very strong shout, which pierces our eardrums, but the monsters don't care and laugh.
He no doubt pierced a cloud at the same time, because it starts to rain.
The monsters lose their colors.
The paper crinkles and shrivels up.
They end up being torn into small bits and tumble into the gutter.
Mom says it's all over. Dad says that, so long as he is in his socks on a slippery roof, nothing is over.

Back home, dad says it's time to say goodbye to Kriss, because he's going to erase him.

We don't want Kriss to be erased. We want him to be with us all the time.

Mom explains to us it's not possible, that Kriss is really nice, but he does too many dumb things.

So, we tell Mom we do dumb things, too and that we're nice.

Mom reflects on it and says, okay then, he can stay with us for good.

We jump with joy, and Kriss knocks over a lamp while doing a tumble.

FULL-LENGTH ADAPTATIONS OF STORIES BY THE WORLD'S GREATEST AUTHORS, BY THE WORLD'S BEST COMIC ARTISTS!

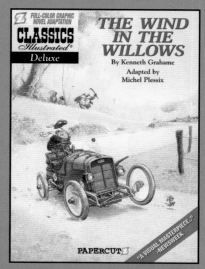

#1 "The Wind In The Willows"

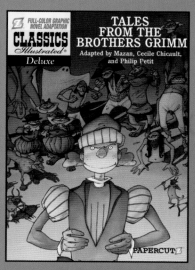

#2 "Tales From The Brothers Grimm"

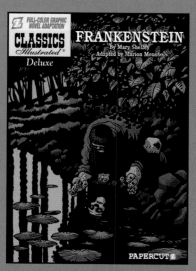

#3 "Frankenstein"

#4 "The Adventures of Tom Sawyer"

#5 "Treasure Island"

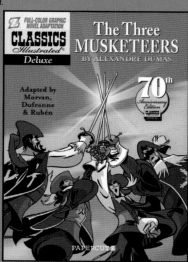

#6 "The Three Musketeers"

WWW.PAPERCUTZ.COM

Take the Trip of a Lifetime-- Without leaving home...

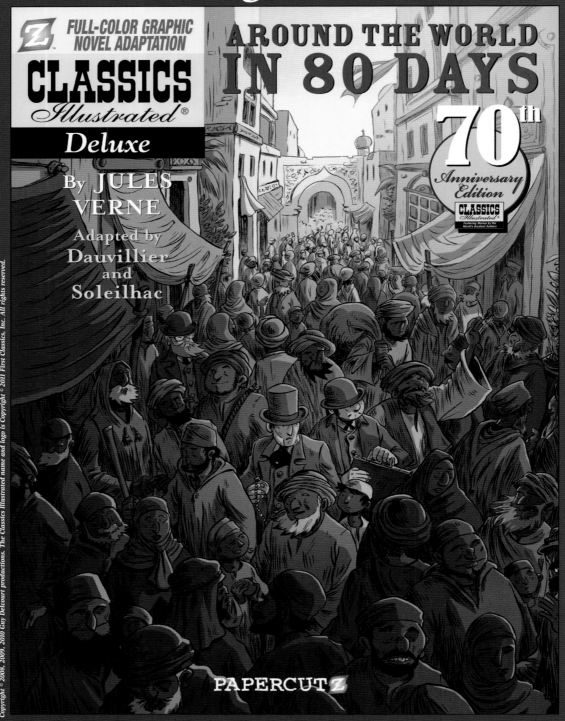